Living Proof Discipleship

Nurturing Your Spiritual Life

in a Way That Influences Others

LEADER'S GUIDE

ZondervanPublishingHouse
Grand Rapids, Michigan

A Division of HarperCollins*Publishers*

CBMC
CHRISTIAN BUSINESS MEN'S COMMITTEE

Living Proof: Discipleship Leader's Guide

First Zondervan edition, 1997

Requests for information should be addressed to:

ZondervanPublishingHouse
Grand Rapids, Michigan 49530

ISBN: 0-310-21389-4

The Christian Business Men's Committee is an international evangelical organization of Christian business and professional men whose primary purpose is to present Jesus Christ as Savior and Lord to other business and professional men and to train these men to carry out the Great Commission (Matthew 28:18-20; Colossians 1:28-29).

CBMC of USA is a nondenominational, nonprofit Christian ministry supported by gifts from people committed to reaching and discipling business and professional men for Jesus Christ. More information may be obtained by writing or calling:

Christian Business Men's Committee of USA
1800 MaCallie Avenue
Chattanooga, TN 37404
615-698-4444

Interior illustrations: Bob Fuller

Printed in the United States of America

96 97 98 99 00 01 02 03 /❖ ML/ 10 9 8 7 6 5 4 3 2 1

Introduction

You are embarking on a journey that Christ traveled. He spent time with the multitudes, but He invested His life with twelve. Those twelve became 120; those 120 became 3000. How did this happen? Through a particular process that Christ modeled for us, and that Paul taught and modeled as well: the process of spiritual reproduction or multiplication. This is not a program, but a process that involves building relationships over a long time.

As parents, we want our children to grow into mature adults who, in turn, will have their own children. Our job is to love and train our children as they grow, so that they will develop into mature adults with godly character qualities, and that, as mature adults, they will go on to accept the privilege and responsibility to parent their own children lovingly and diligently. This is a twenty-year commitment, at least.

Growing up in Christ is a life-long process. The goal is to get to know Christ and to become more like Him—and as we are growing, to help others come to know Christ and help them grow in Him to maturity.

As the leader of this group, you are not signing on for a twenty-year commitment to the members of your group. Still, you'll find yourself practicing some of the qualities of a spiritual parent that the video brings out. Your role in leading this group is to help group members to learn from the video and, just as importantly, to grow in trusting and caring for each other. By the end of the series, we hope at least some members of your group will want to go on to become a team or teams of insiders bringing the gospel to a world of struggling people. We also hope you will find yourself increasingly confident and motivated to become an effective insider and spiritual parent.

SESSION ONE

Christian Growth in the Contemporary Culture

Big Idea: To understand the changing roles of disciple and discipler in today's culture. Discipleship is:
- Process, not programs
- Principles, not methods
- People, not curriculum

The process takes a long time and requires patience because people today are struggling with many issues.

BEFORE THE GROUP GATHERS. Here's a list of things you should do before your first meeting:
- Make sure the TV and VCR are working properly. Are they both plugged in? Are they connected to each other? Do you know how to turn them both on?
- Plan the room format. The ideal for group discussion is a circle, but that makes TV viewing difficult. A semi-circle might work, or some participants could move after the video is turned off. Avoid sitting in rows for discussion.
- Make sure you have copies of the discussion guide for each group member. Please remember that it is illegal to photocopy any portion of the discussion guide to distribute to group members.
- View the video of session 1 yourself.
- Cue the tape to the beginning of session 1, ready for the group to watch it.
- Read through the discussion guide and this leader's guide for session 1.
- Read chapter 1 of *Lifestyle Discipleship* by Jim Petersen. A copy of the book should be in your video kit.

WHEN THE GROUP GATHERS. The main issues group members will be dealing with as they come to this first session are, "Is this topic relevant to me?" "Is this group worth my time?" and "Will I fit in?" Your job is to help them feel comfortable and see why they should invest part of their busy schedules in this course.

Allow about ten minutes for everyone to get a cup of coffee and get situated in the room. Then begin, even if some people are late, so those present won't feel their time is being wasted.

Pages 5-6 of the discussion guide ("What Is This Series About?") sketch out for the group what will happen in each session. People usually like to know what to expect, so after opening in prayer, allow a minute or two to read over the introductory information silently or aloud. Invite any questions about what is going to happen. Point out that photos of each of the main characters are on pages 5-6 to help participants remember the characters' names and who is married to whom.

QUESTIONS 1 and 2. These questions are designed to help participants focus on the topic at hand and share some of their own experiences. Sharing their own stories will help them feel more comfortable and get to know each other better. Hearing their stories will help you know what issues from the course will be most relevant for each participant. Limit this storytelling to fifteen minutes, however, or you won't have enough time to discuss the video. You can model an appropriate level of sharing by answering questions 1 or 2 before the rest of the group.

Question 1 is appropriate if you think most of your group members have had some experience with the term *discipleship*. If you think most participants will be unfamiliar with this term, then use question 2. The latter question could help you enormously in understanding the particular needs of each group member. You might decide to discuss both questions. However, don't allow talking before the video to prevent adequate discussion after the video. Participants may decide not to come back for the next session if they think the group is making no progress.

VIDEO. Most people are accustomed to watching television passively, just letting the images wash over them. Studies have shown that after twenty-five minutes of continuous television viewing, our brain waves actually slow down and our visual perspective narrows. Since this is a teaching video, one of your goals will be to help participants watch actively, with their brains fully turned on. There are two things you can do to encourage active viewing:

- Adequately prepare the group for what they will watch.
- Give participants an assignment to focus on while watching.

This opening segment, in particular, merits adequate introduction. The story flashes from the present (in the cabin) to several years in the past (when Gerry fights with Erik, and the men's and women's groups each meet for lunch). You should view the segment before the group meeting, so you know what to expect. Then, after the warm-up questions and before you turn the tape on, read aloud the introduction to this segment on page 7 of the discussion guide, or use your own words to summarize what participants are about to see. Make sure everyone understands that the cabin scenes are in the present and the other scenes are flashbacks.

Finally, ask participants to take notes on the question under "Your Notes from the Video." This will be one of the first questions you will discuss after turning the tape off.

One theme of this session and those that follow is *brokenness*. Most people today come to Christ broken in some way, with some significant pain about relationships, job, etc. Some are all too aware of their pain; others manage to numb their pain with alcohol, drugs, sexual behavior, food, overwork, busyness, compulsive religious activity, and other strategies. Consequently, some in your group may be like Gerry, Linda, Bill, and Jackie—very aware that children or finances are causing them great pain—while others may be more like Steve, who in a later session admits that for years he ignored his pain and tried to power through everything. Those like Steve may not identify with *brokenness*. They may not feel broken at all. That's okay; it's not the purpose of this video to push people to feel pain they don't feel.

QUESTION 4. Some in the video, such as Erik, Alice, and Mary Beth, are not yet Christians at the time of the fight between Gerry and Erik. For them, the major issue is, "What do I think about Christ and Christians?" We normally think of this as an "evangelism" issue, not a "discipleship" issue, but in *Lifestyle Discipleship*, Jim Petersen argues that evangelism and discipleship are part of the same continuum. Session 3 will address this more fully.

Family relations stand at the head of Gerry's issues as a new believer. Linda also has questions about money. As more mature believers, Bill and Jackie are not only dealing with major personal issues—tight finances, the pressure for Jackie to work, losing their house, busyness—but are also facing the question, "How do we help Gerry and Linda grow?" As time goes on, we'll see how older believers help younger believers grow, and how younger believers—and even not-yet believers—play key roles in each person's growth. Gerry looks to Bill to *model* what life in Christ is all about; how is Bill doing?

Draw attention to the character issues each person faces: anger, resentment, self-control, patience, mercy, pride. As later sessions show, these are the key issues of Christian growth, more fundamental than mere mastery of Bible knowledge or skills.

You can also catch a glimpse of an issue that will turn up again and again: busyness. Session 11 will focus on this, but point it out now. Many participants will probably identify with this struggle.

QUESTION 5. Your group may find it very easy to identify with Gerry and Linda's struggles with parenting, or with Bill and Jackie's financial problems. On the other hand, you could ask group members to make their own lists of issues. Using a white board or sheet of newsprint, write down the group's answers to a question such as one of these:

- What are some of the hot issues people today struggle with as they seek to grow in Christ?
- What are some of the hot issues you struggle with as you seek to grow in Christ?

The first of these questions is less personal than the second and might be more appropriate if your group members don't know each other well enough to answer the second question frankly.

Some in your group may find it hard to identify with people struggling as much as those in this video. They may have pictures in their minds of "broken" people as pathetic, weak, unrespectable. However, are Bill and Jackie weak, pathetic people just because they are struggling with the aftermath of a job loss? Are Gerry and Linda incapable of helping others grow because they need to grow a lot in the area of parenting? One theme of this series is that all of us are weak in some ways, and all of us also are strong through Christ to make a huge difference in our world. The struggling people in this video are also called and gifted people with a lot to offer those around them. Talk about this idea of being both broken and strong with your group if you think it will be helpful.

QUESTION 6. Some participants may have had experience with some of these old assumptions, such as the notion that "serious" disciples show up on time with their homework done. Ask if anyone can identify with the idea of "moving with the movers" or "commitment to the program is commitment to Christ."

Other participants may have had no experience with this older model of discipleship and may find it foreign. Allow them to express their feelings about it.

SESSION TWO

It's an Inside Job

Big Idea: God calls us to grow in Christ while remaining insiders among the unbelievers in our workplaces, neighborhoods, and families. God wants to use us right where we are.

BEFORE YOU MEET:

- View the video of session 2.
- Cue the tape back to the beginning of session 2.
- Read the discussion guide and this leader's guide for session 2.
- Read chapter 2 of *Lifestyle Discipleship*.

Most members of your group will probably never have thought of themselves as insiders strategically placed by God in their homes, workplaces, and neighborhoods. Being an insider is sometimes tough, but it can also be encouraging to know that God has called us and wants to use us right where we are. Your goal in this session should be to help participants get excited about the idea of being insiders, while facing the potential challenges.

An effective insider pursues relationships with nonChristians and is willing to be vulnerable about his or her weaknesses. Unbelievers don't need to see us as perfect; they need to watch while Jesus changes us. It's hard for many of us to grasp that transparency, rather than a pretense of perfection, is what we should be showing others, so you may want to emphasize it. Talk about how it affects you, as a believer, when other believers are honest about their struggles and you can see how God is at work in their lives. Do you prefer to live around seemingly "perfect" Christians or around those who are struggling alongside you? Discuss with group members whether they are willing to let people see their struggles. You can set a good example by being willing to share your struggles with your group.

QUESTION 6. Some of the forces that hinder us from being effective insiders are: fear; the desire to stay in a comfortable, Christian world; poor counsel from well-meaning Christians; indifference toward unbelievers; and busyness. Ask group members to tell which forces are the biggest problems for each of them. Then discuss ways of addressing those problems. (See question 10c.)

QUESTION 8. This question addresses one of the main objections to leaving a new believer with his relationships intact: "Those old friends will drag him back to worldly living!" There are cases when old ties should be broken; for instance, persons addicted to chemicals or homosexual sex usually need to be separated from practicing addicts until they are securely free from their addictions. However, the Holy Spirit, regular input from the Scriptures, and a few solid, honest relationships with mature believers can go a long way toward keeping most young believers on the right path in the midst of their old relationships. It's important for a new believer to have at least one safe, mature, nonjudgmental friend with whom to talk openly about temptation. Gerry had Bill and Steve to help him grow while remaining an insider.

QUESTION 11. This question is essential. If you run out of time in this session to talk about question 11, consider spending your next meeting on it. Take time to let each group member respond to questions a-d, and talk about each person's situation. You may not be able to solve all of the problems no, but do write down a list of everyone's questions, concerns, frustrations, or needs. Later sessions may address many questions. You'll be returning to this question repeatedly throughout the series.

SESSION THREE

The Path to Maturity

Big Idea: Spiritual parents help disciples grow through stages of infancy, childhood, adolescence, and adulthood. We all need spiritual parents when we are new in faith, and we all can be spiritual parents to someone else.

BEFORE YOU MEET:

- View the video of session 3.
- Cue the tape back to the beginning of session 3.
- Read the discussion guide and this leader's guide for session 3.
- Read chapters 3 and 4 of *Lifestyle Discipleship.*

QUESTION 4. Spiritual parenting is the key theme of this session. Some participants may never have had a spiritual parent, while others may have. Allow participants to share a bit of their own experience as well as their feelings about spiritual parenting. Invite others to respond. For instance, someone might say, "I never had a spirtual parent, and I'm doing fine spiritually." Ask others whether they think this person's experience shows that spiritual parenting is unnecessary. Share your own experience of having or being a spiritual parent, or of never having had or been one.

The video emphasizes the shift from a farming metaphor for evangelism to a parenting metaphor for disciplemaking. One shouldn't press metaphors too far, but it's important to understand that disciples don't just grow naturally; they require lots of care and personal attention to grow up healthy.

QUESTION 7. Participants who have had negative experiences with their natural parents will naturally have some negative images come to mind when they think of spiritual parents. Mention this fact, and invite participants to share any misgivings they may have about spiritual parents. For instance, some might feel that a spiritual parent sounds like someone who dominates and controls others. Contrast this impression with what the video portrays. The video stresses that spiritual parents and children are on parallel growth paths, both are growing and struggling, no one has "arrived." A possible question after question 6 might be, "Mary Beth finds the parenting image painful because of her own experience with parents. Can you identify with her concern? If so, how?"

QUESTION 8. Compare the ideal growth path of the Critical Process with other possible paths, such as the two in the margin on page 19. What has your path looked like?

You may want to avoid digressing into a discussion of whether it's possible to fall off the path totally. This is a matter of intense theological debate that would require more space and time than this session allows.

QUESTIONS 10 and 12. These questions allow participants to tell what they think they need from the group or other sources. Pay close attention to their answers. How can you facilitate the group giving maximum help to its members? What other resources can you offer participants?

ADDITIONAL QUESTIONS. How does the spiritual parent's role change as the disciple matures? How long do you think it takes for a person to grow from spiritual birth to adulthood? Most of us acknowledge that maturity takes years.

ACTION STEPS. Consider brainstorming a list of ways group members can act as insiders. Talk about ways you've been an insider, or talk about your own struggles to be an insider. Is it hard for you to build significant relationships with nonChristians? What gets in the way? What have been some of the joys of spiritual parenting for you?

SESSION FOUR

What Changes Fast, What Changes Slowly

Big Idea: Some things change immediately when we trust Christ. Other things change very slowly, over years. We need to be patient with ourselves, our spiritual children, and our sisters and brothers. Community is critical for Christian growth—it takes a whole village to raise a child.

BEFORE YOU MEET:

- View the video of session 4.
- Cue the tape back to the beginning of session 4.
- Read the discussion guide and this leader's guide for session 4.
- Read chapter 5 of *Lifestyle Discipleship*.

QUESTION 4. Here are some of the key points about change that this session makes, in addition to those noted in the discussion guide:

- Maturity takes time, a lot of time.
- The important thing is progress, not instant perfection.
- Change isn't just about doing all the right stuff.
- Being real is more important than looking good.
- The battlegrounds of growth are the mind and the body.
- Sin's power is broken, but it hangs on because "it knows its way around" in our lives.
- The Holy Spirit is our chief ally, the main agent of change.
- We have to yield to the Spirit's influence.
- Spiritual disciplines train our minds and bodies in the same way that physical disciplines train an athlete for competition.
- What we do flows out of who we are—life change is based on character.
- Staying focused on Christ protects us from legalism and the narrowness of any particular religious tradition.
- Christ changes our motives for doing what we do.
- Community is essential for growth; "it takes a whole village to raise a child."
- Problems often get worse before they get better as we dig for the roots of those problems.

Depending on how much of this list emerges from group discussion of question 3, you can select among questions 4-7. You may not need to discuss each of them individually. Select those that seem most important for your group.

QUESTIONS 8-10. Questions 8 and 10 are sandwiched around question 9. Question 9 is a more directive, leading question, while 8 and 10 are more open-ended. You can decide how much time you want to give to this topic, and whether you prefer to be directive or open-ended. Don't feel you need to discuss all of these questions.

QUESTION 11. This question recalls your earlier discussion about spiritual parenting. You probably don't need to spend much time on it; just briefly draw attention to the fact that helping Thomas actually helps Raz. We keep returning to this concept because many Christians find it surprising. They have always assumed that they need to mature before they help someone else. Romans 1:12 says even the apostle Paul grew from encouragement from those he served.

ACTION STEPS. For you, the most important question may be the last one: Do you provide a safe environment that encourages others to share with you?

SESSION FIVE

Change from the Inside Out

Big Idea: God wants us to change from the inside out. Behind everyone's story (external behavior) there's a story (what's happened to him or her in the past, what's happening inside him or her now). Instead of focusing on changing behavior (ours or that of our spiritual children) we need to focus on changing world view and values.

BEFORE YOU MEET:

- View the video of session 5.
- Cue the tape back to the beginning of session 5.
- Read the discussion guide and this leader's guide for session 5.
- Read chapter 6 of *Lifestyle Discipleship.*

You may also want to review concepts from sessions 1 through 4 that are illustrated by this session's drama: struggling people helping struggling people; spiritual parenting; community; the process of change. How do Bill, Gerry, and the others demonstrate the principles of discipleship that you've already learned?

QUESTIONS 4 and 5. "World view" and "values" seem like unreachable abstract concepts to many people at first, so we've tried to give you something concrete to focus on: Gerry's situation. You could just as well discuss Raz's situation or that of another character if you prefer. The answer to question 4 is that Gerry can't change his behavior by willpower because his behavior is driven less by his surface, conscious will than by beliefs and values he's barely aware of. Sin has clouded his reason and feelings so that he doesn't perceive or understand reality clearly. According to Matthew 13:15, humans have chosen to grow callouses on their hearts and to close their eyes to reality, so it's no wonder we can't just decide one day to think clearly and do what's right. Softening our hearts is a long process of cooperation with the Holy Spirit over years.

Some members of your group may be very aware of their inner worlds: the thoughts and feelings most people never see. They may also find it easy to infer from Gerry's behavior what is probably going on inside him. Other participants may find this more difficult. To some extent, this is a difference of natural gifts (some people are just more inwardly attuned and intuitive than others). However, all of us can develop our ability to look beneath surface behavior to see the story behind the story. Encourage participants who find it difficult to talk about feelings and values that they can grow in this area, and that it's important that they do so.

QUESTION 6. If participants have trouble with this question, work through it with question 8. The point is the same as in question 4: we often lack the power to treat people with love, to not get angry, or to say the right thing on the spur of the moment because those behaviors are fueled by our values and world-view beliefs. Gerry is a classic case. Paul makes it clear in Colossians that he understands this fact. Spiritual disciplines have value in training our minds and bodies if we address those disciplines to our values and beliefs, not if we simply do spiritual disciplines as new behaviors and then try to control the rest of our behavior through willpower.

QUESTION 7. The Bible is the ideal source of a Christ-centered world view. A community of other believers who are honestly wrestling with their own world views, values, and behaviors is also essential; only very rare people can integrate biblical truth in isolation.

QUESTION 8. Paul describes the shift in beliefs and values as setting our minds on things above, rather than on earthly things. In other words, we need to view our world from God's perspective ("above") rather than from a typical human perspective. Paul says this as an instruction, something we are capable of doing, but he is under no illusions that we can do it instantaneously or easily. This shift is a process that will take time and effort.

Question 8c is another opportunity to see how world view determines behavior. If Gerry viewed his life as being with Christ rather than as depending on anything Erik does, then Gerry would have much less reason to be explosively angry about Erik. Gerry's anger is what blocks him from choosing to treat Erik with love. Gerry can't just choose not to be angry, but if he really believed his life was with Christ rather than fragilely dependent upon Erik's obedience, then that belief would drain his anger.

Question 8d is an opportunity to emphasize that setting our minds on things above requires time and effort. Gerry needs to meditate on the truth: that his worth as a person comes from being made in God's image and filled with the Holy Spirit, not from anything Erik does. His friends can help him remember this, but ultimately he needs to pray for the Holy Spirit to help him live by it.

QUESTION 9. Focusing on behavior is a lot easier than looking inside ourselves to figure out what's really going on. It takes work to figure out the story behind the story, especially for those of us not naturally gifted at doing this. However, it's a skill we can learn.

QUESTION 10. Reasons include pride and selfishness, as well as the knowledge that it's often not safe to discuss our sin with others. We may know others are not trustworthy because they will judge us, gossip, or abuse information in some other way. We may know they will look only at behavior and not help in the pursuit of the story behind the story. Explore this as a group, and talk about what a safe place for honesty would look like. Talk about what you like in the relationships portrayed in the video.

QUESTION 11. Don't push this, but give participants an opportunity to share what they're thinking and feeling. Probably most people can identify with Gerry and Raz and the rest in some way: we see behaviors we don't like, but digging beneath them to our motives looks like a lot of work. It may feel overwhelming, frustrating, encouraging, or discouraging. Your group can start being a safe place in which to help each other find the story behind each of your stories.

SESSION SIX

Sin, the Worst Deal in Town

Big Idea: We sin . . .
- because it's in our nature to sin
- because we program ourselves with sinful habits
- because we have blind spots in areas where truth would be uncomfortable

Repentance means deciding to change direction; it's a decision of the will that requires dependence upon the Holy Spirit to carry out. We can help each other in this process by being open about our own weaknesses and providing a safe environment for confession.

BEFORE YOU MEET:

- View the video of session 6.
- Cue the tape back to the beginning of session 6.
- Read the discussion guide and this leader's guide for session 6.
- Read chapter 7 of *Lifestyle Discipleship.*

Don't just use this session as a chance for participants to learn information about sin. Use it as an opportunity for them to experience stopping, asking for help, and changing direction. Your group meeting may or may not be an appropriate place for everyone to bare his or her soul, but you can set a powerful example by telling some of your story. What's an area of sin in your life that you've struggled with during the past five years? You may not need to give all the details about how you've sinned, but do talk about how you've dealt with this issue. Have you prayed? What happened? Have you talked with anyone? Has wise counsel been helpful? Have the Scriptures helped? Has there been pain or frustration in the process? What about joy or victory? Paint an honest picture for your group. By doing this, you'll give struggling group members the kind of freedom Steve gives to Raz to open up in this session's video segment. You may find that someone in your group is a Raz and needs to talk to you.

QUESTION 2. Raz learned three reasons why sin continues to grip even though God's Spirit lives in him. He also learned that he's not the only one of his friends struggling with sin. Knowing we're not alone is enormously important. Further, he learned that Bill can honestly say he's making progress; we all need that encouragement that it's not hopeless! And Raz learned some of the resources available to him: the Holy Spirit, the Scriptures, and even his friends. Many of us think we're on our own; make sure your group sees how essential Bill, Steve, and the others are in Raz's process of growth.

QUESTION 3. Discuss the implications of the car image. It's a mistake to push an analogy too far, but the car image makes some helpful points. First, it's up to us to stop the car. God won't do that for us; otherwise, we'd be robots. Second, there's no shame in asking for directions. In fact, not asking for directions is just plain arrogant and foolish. Prayer, reading the Bible, reading other books, and talking to fellow believers are all forms of asking for directions. Third, admitting we're lost is essential, and God never condemns us for being lost. He's thrilled when we admit it, and happy to help us turn around. But we have to actually turn around, not just think about turning around or wish we could turn around. We'll mess up frequently, and doing so shouldn't discourage us, but we need to keep deciding again to turn around.

QUESTION 6. For Raz, offering himself to God might look like many things. For instance, it might include canceling his post office box, agreeing with Steve to check in together once a week on how the pornography struggle is going, reading a book on sexual addiction, and/or setting aside some time to think and write about "Why does pornography seem more appealing to me than a real sexual relationship with my wife?"

SESSION SEVEN

No Left Turn

Big Idea: Spiritual transformation occurs as we struggle with our experiences in light of God's Word and among community. It's essential in this process to choose the right turn through humility and dependence on the Holy Spirit, rather than the left turn to self-control through willpower.

BEFORE YOU MEET:

- View the video of session 7.
- Cue the tape back to the beginning of session 7.
- Read the discussion guide and this leader's guide for session 7.
- Read chapter 8 of *Lifestyle Discipleship.*

You'll want to emphasize these questions:

- What are the seven elements?
- What examples of this process do you see in the lives of the video characters?
- How do you see this process at work in your own lives?

While all seven elements are important, we've chosen to focus on the one most often overlooked: *humility.* Humility makes the difference between the right turn and the left turn, between access to the Holy Spirit's power and the lack of it. Humility is much misunderstood; people confuse it with shame, shyness, lack of self-respect, and so on. The other elements—such as community, the Scriptures, and the Holy Spirit—turn up over and over in this video series, but this is the one session where you'll have a chance to focus on humility.

To help participants fully grasp the process of transformation from experience to self-control, you can refer back to the seven elements in future sessions.

QUESTION 1. The warm-up question has to do with forgiveness, because it refers back to the Action Step in session 6 and because it offers a measure of humility, one of the most important elements of spiritual transformation. Think about your own answer ahead of time. Are you in the habit of asking forgiveness—not apologizing for everything and living constantly under the pressure of guilt and trying to please people, but genuine, humble restoration of relationship when you've hurt someone?

QUESTION 2. If your time is limited, select just a few of these points to cover. Here is one example of each point:

- Their experience of parenting a hostile teenager is forcing both Gerry and Linda to face their desire to control others and themselves.
- It's up to Gerry to choose whether his experience with Erik will make him more loving and compassionate, or more angry.
- Reading Romans 6–8 helped Raz understand why his addiction to pornography was so powerful and how he should address it.
- Just reading Romans didn't end the struggle for Raz; he still felt the war between what would give him life and what seemed to feel good.
- As long as Gerry keeps trying to control his anger at Erik without humbling himself, he'll keep failing.
- The Holy Spirit affected Raz's ethics at work enough to catch Thomas's attention.
- Throwing out one magazine was a good start for Raz, but not the end of the battle.
- Linda probably wouldn't be able to keep from totally hiding from her family by working if it weren't for the women's lunch group, where the other women ask her straight questions and encourage her.

QUESTIONS 4 and 5. If participants don't jump to answer these questions, you can set the tone by answering them yourself. Think ahead of time about what level of self-revelation is appropriate in your group. What information about your own current growth process can your members handle?

QUESTION 6. Surprisingly, beating up on oneself reflects an arrogant attitude. When we do this, we arrogantly refuse to admit we need either God's forgiveness or His power, and we refuse to receive either of them. Self-punishment assumes that we can make ourselves do right. Humility is a much more joyful stance; it gratefully receives what God offers.

SESSION EIGHT

God Doesn't Waste Pain

Big Idea: Growth most often occurs in the context of painful experiences. God never abandons us in those times; He is always there to comfort and strengthen us through them.

BEFORE YOU MEET:

- View the video of session 8.
- Cue the tape back to the beginning of session 8.
- Read the discussion guide and this leader's guide for session 8.
- Read chapter 9 of *Lifestyle Discipleship.*

This session could feel depressing unless you use it as a chance to deal constructively with pain and sadness group members might be feeling. Watching the video characters talk about their pain will naturally touch painful spots for some group members. Seize the chance to support one another as the video characters support each other.

QUESTION 2. Everyone is sad sometimes; sadness is part of life in a sinful world. People who never feel sad are usually doing something less-than-healthy to numb their feelings. It is true that there are a wide variety of healthy ways to handle sadness, depending on our personalities. Some people benefit from time alone to think; others benefit from talking with people. But if a person avoids ever being alone in order to avoid the feelings of sadness that might well up, then there's a problem.

Don't pass judgment on participants' answers to this question, but do listen. You may get clues as to who might need help in handling pain.

QUESTIONS 6-9. Think about your own answers to these questions before the group meets. What can you share that will invite others to open up? Do you tend to be like Steve, an excellent group leader, but one more comfortable talking about others' needs than his own? When Steve tells his story about his dad's death, it powerfully affects his friend. Talk about your own struggles.

SESSION NINE

When Life Is Messy

Big Idea: A constructive response to our own suffering involves humbly depending on God for strength to endure, and humbly receiving comfort from other people. A constructive response to another person's suffering involves standing with them, not giving advice.

BEFORE YOU MEET:

- View the video of session 9.
- Cue the tape back to the beginning of session 9.
- Read the discussion guide and this leader's guide for session 9.
- Read chapter 10 of *Lifestyle Discipleship*.

This session is about how to respond to our own and others' pain. The video characters model some good responses; the discussion guide questions offer you a chance to do the same for each other in your group.

QUESTION 2. Draw attention to the healthy balance between taking responsibility for one's own life and relying on others. On one hand, the characters take time alone to pray, feel their emotions, and take appropriate action. They're not whining victims. On the other hand, they call their friends and depend on their friends for emotional support.

QUESTION 3. Again, notice how the characters care for one another without treating each other like helpless children. They sense how to be warmly involved without meddling or controlling.

QUESTION 6. This question is a bit of a tangent to the topic of suffering, but it's a reminder that we're trying to make discipleship work for people in the "secular" arena, where they can continue to influence nonChristians.

QUESTION 7. Be sensitive to how much probing each group member needs. In some cases, you may want to pursue someone to talk more about a struggle he is facing. Some people need a direct, gentle invitation to talk about what they need because they're not used to saying, "I need" or "I would like." One of the goals of this series is to give viewers permission to be both strong and weak in front of other people, just as the video characters are sometimes weak and sometimes strong in Christ.

QUESTION 8. Use this question as a springboard to talk about what practical help you can be to each other, as well as what your limitations are. Listening and caring can be valuable gifts, even when you can't do more. The video characters made time in their schedules and room in their hearts just to be with each other during a painful situation. But time is a huge barrier for many people. You've already begun to see how time is a problem for Bill; you'll be discussing that head-on in session 11.

SESSION TEN

Character, Community, and Competence

Big Idea: Character is the end product of growth. Community is the context in which significant growth takes place. Competence, including skills and knowledge, is a set of tools for growth.

BEFORE YOU MEET:

- View the video of session 10.
- Cue the tape back to the beginning of session 10.
- Read the discussion guide and this leader's guide for session 10.
- Read chapter 11 of *Lifestyle Discipleship*.

QUESTION 3. Losing her house and having to take a job have humbled Jackie. She's not humiliated in the sense of feeling ashamed; rather, she's learned not to care what people think about her status. She's more secure in Christ, more able to care for someone else.

Linda has learned to lead from vulnerability. She's stopped trying to control and change Gerry and Erik, and she's stopped hiding from them at work. She's telling them the truth kindly, showing them how they affect her without punishing them.

Gerry has learned he can't control his anger on his own; he needs God. He's learned to humble himself even in front of Erik. He's listening to his wife instead of giving her ultimatums.

All three have learned humility, and humility is leading to growth in other aspects of their characters. They are growing in faith (believing that Christ really is who the Bible says He is), hope (believing God will care for them even when circumstances are agonizing), and love (the ability to allow others access to their hearts and to give others what they really need).

QUESTION 4. Community has provided them with a safe, caring place to face their character and faith issues: Mary Beth's doubts about God, Gerry's anger at Erik, and Linda's anger at Gerry. Community has provided them with accountability: they can't hide from their problems. But that accountability isn't pressure to conform; it's loving and respectful. The community has won the right to tell them the tough truth because it has shared their pain. It has encouraged them to grow in competencies like Bible knowledge, provided a place for worship, and fostered their unique spiritual gifts. One of the main clues that this community is healthy is that Mary Beth came into it as an unbeliever and was fully accepted, with all her doubts and questions, and slowly drawn to Christ. A healthy community attracts people to Christ; a community that isn't attracting unbelievers should ask itself what is missing.

QUESTION 5. See the list in question 4. These are the kinds of things a healthy community can do to foster growth. These features are essential. Because most character issues have to do with relationships, God has designed the Body of Christ to be interdependent. We simply don't grow as well on our own. But the community has to be a safe place that builds people up, not a critical, demanding place that tears them down. It has to reflect God's character accurately; people have to see grace at work, not legalism.

You might add the question, "Is our group this kind of growth-fostering community? What are our strengths and weaknesses?" Hopefully, you've provided a safe environment in which group members can answer this honestly. Skip this question if you think it will make you or other group members uncomfortable.

QUESTION 7. Consider answering this question yourself first, and think about what you want to say ahead of time. Your answer will model for the group the way they should approach the question. For instance, let's say you want to grow in resolving conflict in a way that respects both yourself and the other person, rather than being overcome with anger. That's a character issue. Community could help you by providing a safe place for you to come clean about the way you are relating to your spouse, your kids, or your coworkers. It could provide a place where you see how others handle conflict. It could help you dig down to the roots of your anger: What really sparks your anger? Is it when you don't feel respected, or when you feel out of control? What's the root issue that God wants to address? Community can provide a place for you to think this through. By loving you even when you fail, the people in your community can help you keep confessing failure without giving up.

Suffering may be both one of the reasons why you're angry and a catalyst for growth. Maybe strife with your spouse or someone you've been dating is what is finally forcing you to take a hard look at the way you relate and humble yourself enough for God to go to work.

Growth in this area will take soul-searching, maybe journaling, exploring what the Bible says about anger and conflict resolution, much prayer and time and struggle. It will take a lot of right turns through humility and a fair amount of asking for forgiveness.

QUESTION 8. A spiritual parent can help a person learn what the Bible says about character growth in general as well as about a particular issue. The parent can do the kinds of things Steve did for Raz: ask probing questions, provide a safe place for confession, point toward the Scriptures, encourage the despairing, and nudge the complacent. Ask, "What do natural parents do to help their children grow in character?"

SESSION ELEVEN

Running on Empty

Big Idea: Both spiritual parenting and personal growth require time. We will never be effective as Insiders unless we address chronic busyness.

BEFORE YOU MEET:

- View the video of session 11.
- Cue the tape back to the beginning of session 11.
- Read the discussion guide and this leader's guide for session 11.
- Read chapter 13 of *Lifestyle Discipleship.*

Many people find this to be the most important session of the series. If we don't solve our problem with overcommitment and consequent exhaustion, we'll have neither the time nor the inner resources to give to others. All this talk of insiders, spiritual parents, and personal growth will be for naught. But solving the overcommitment problem is no small task, and it probably won't happen in one group session. Your goal in this session should be to frame the issue so that everyone in the group understands it as critical—not merely because overcommitment damages us (although it does) or makes people mad at us, but because it blocks us from doing what is most important in life.

It would be worth your while to read *Margin* by Dr. Richard Swenson. Draw participants' attention to the response postcard in their discussion guides; it offers a copy of *Margin* to any participant who sends an address to CBMC.

QUESTION 2. The key here is that Bill is overloaded because his priorities are askew. It's easy for us to think our stress comes from all the things we have to do. While it's true that in a time of economic uncertainty we may have to work long hours, some of us are working long hours in the pursuit of career success, money to support a lifestyle beyond the essentials, or even (like Linda) an escape from disappointments at home. Likewise, some of our busyness at church may not be what God really desires from us. When we don't have time for our families or the lost world around us, we have to ask ourselves, "What's wrong?" And often what's wrong is that we are allowing cultural values, rather than God's values, to determine our priorities.

QUESTION 7. Ideally, your group has grown to trust one another well enough to talk openly about your lives. You might take each individual or couple one by one, and let them share the pressures they see hindering them from having the energy to give to being God's representatives for others. If you have trouble getting the discussion rolling, consider laying out your own situation for the group first. What obstacles do you face? Invite help in sorting out your own priorities.

ACTION STEPS. Encourage participants to set some dates to get away and assess their lives. Set an example by scheduling your own retreat time and telling the group about your plans.

SESSION TWELVE

The Eternal Purpose

Big Idea: We can live on the seventy-year plan, as though this life is all there is, or we can devote our lives to something that has value for eternity.

BEFORE YOU MEET:

- View the video of session 12.
- Cue the tape back to the beginning of session 12.
- Read the discussion guide and this leader's guide for session 12.
- Read chapter 12 of *Lifestyle Discipleship*.

This should be an upbeat, encouraging, motivating session. Your goal here should be to summarize what you've covered in this series, find out what each participant will take away from it, and encourage participants to do something with what they've learned. The best thing you can do is be candid about what you plan to do with what you have learned, as well as about the areas where you are still struggling. How motivated are you to be an Insider?

QUESTION 4. This question is not intended to criticize people who choose to work on church staffs. That's an honorable calling. Rather, it is intended to help participants who work and live in a "secular" arena realize that their calling is essential to the functioning of the Church.